Soledad Bravi

Mommy, Pick Me Up

FARRAR STRAUS GIROUX

NEW YORK

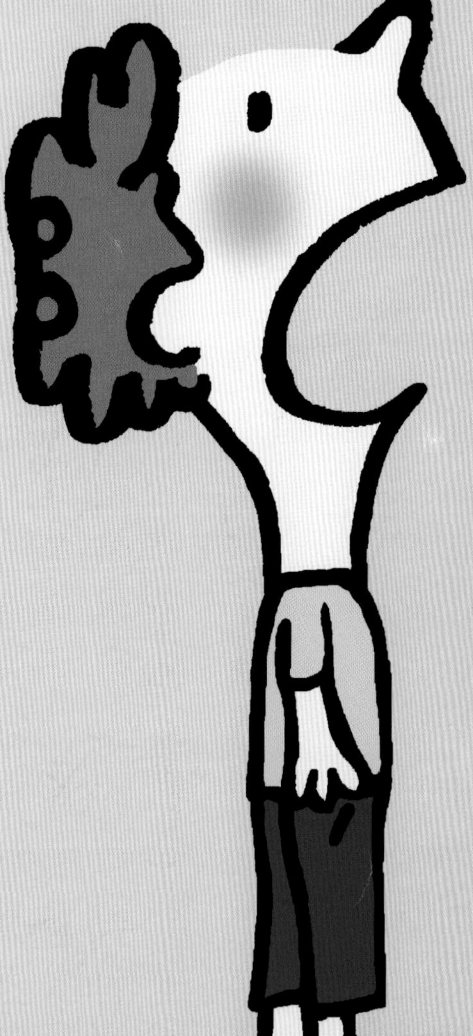

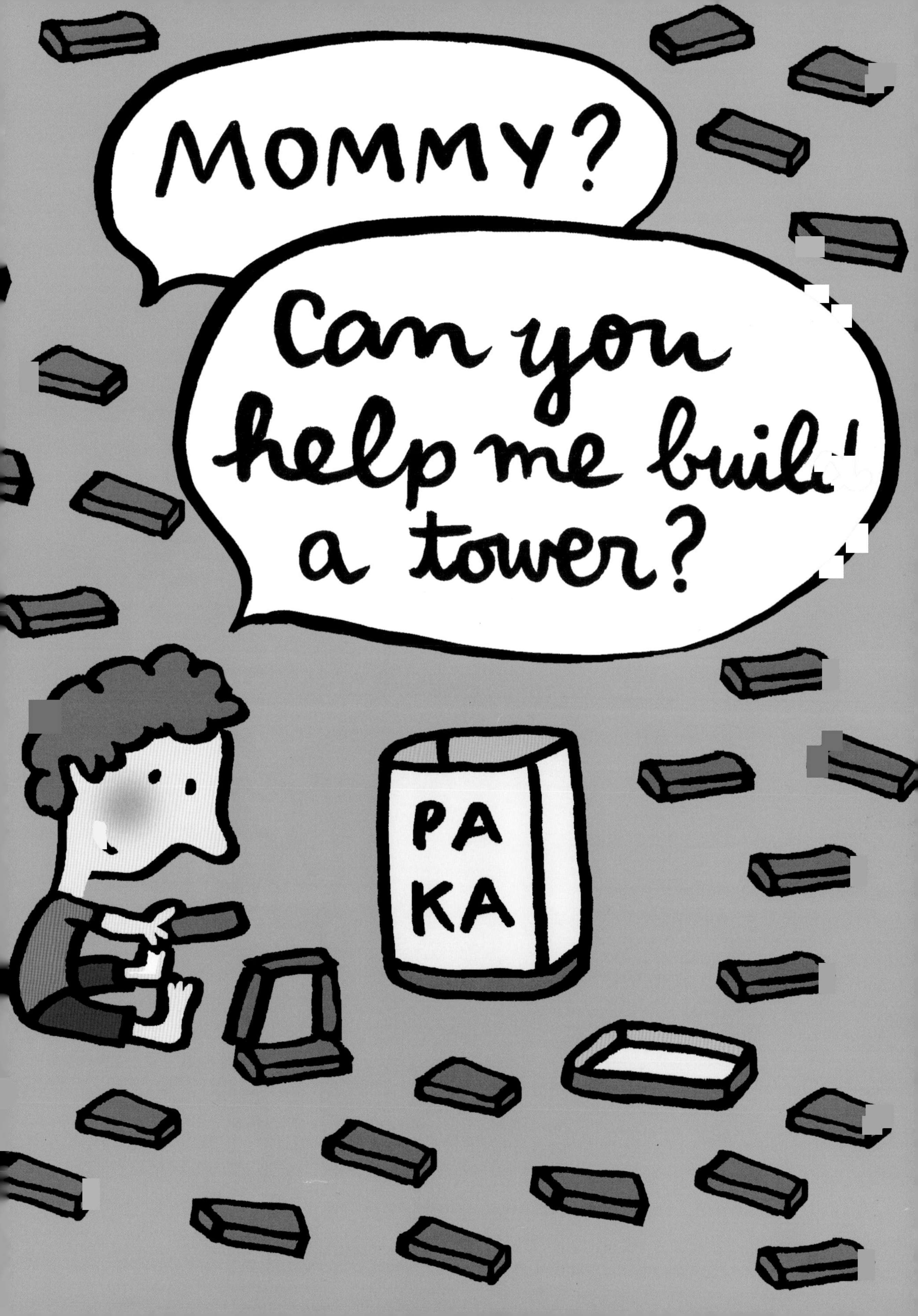
MOMMY?
Can you help me buil
a tower?
PA KA

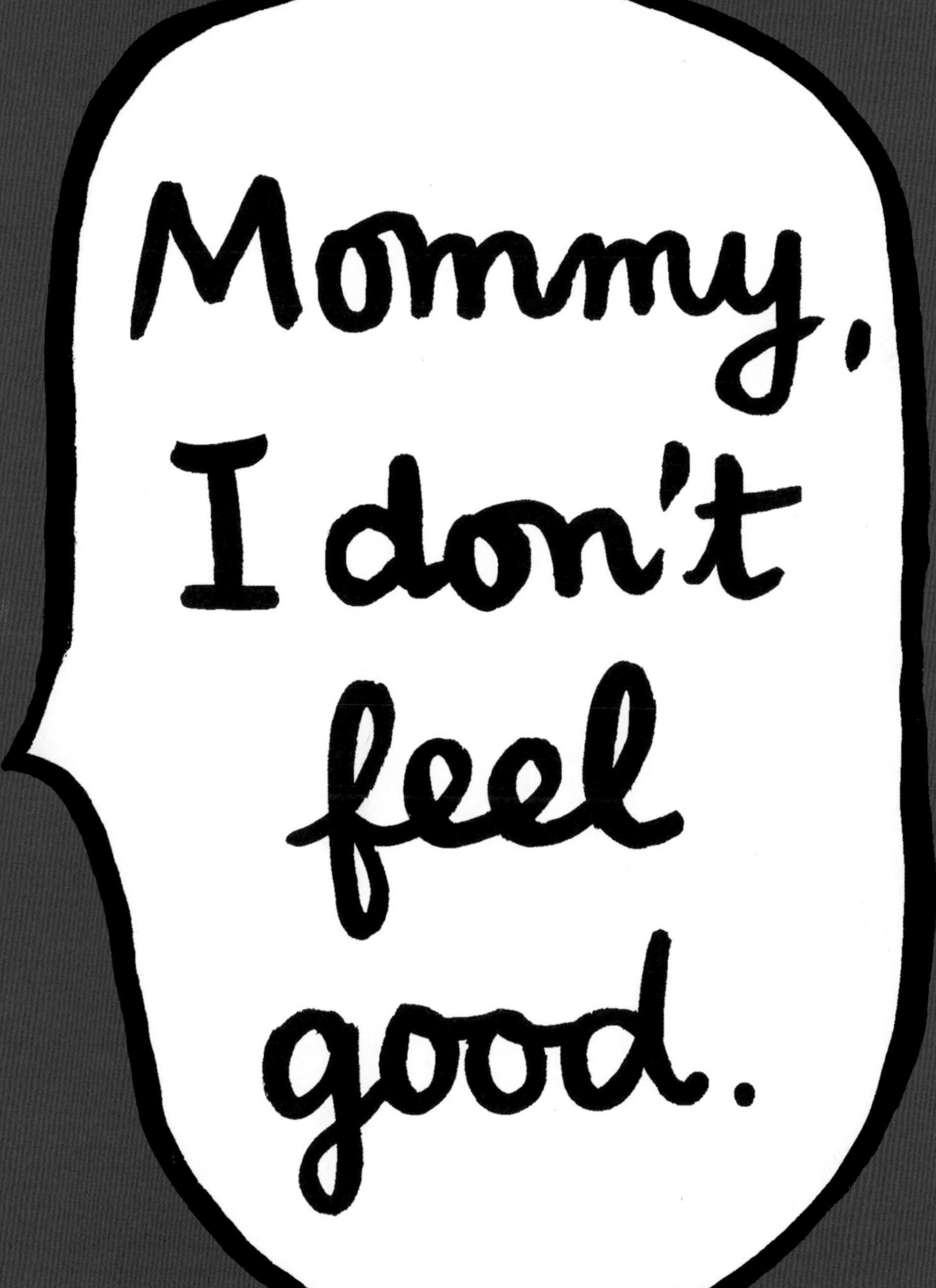
Mommy, I don't feel good.

on
lap?

MOMMY,
your
phone is
moving...

Mommy, can I help you crack the eggs?

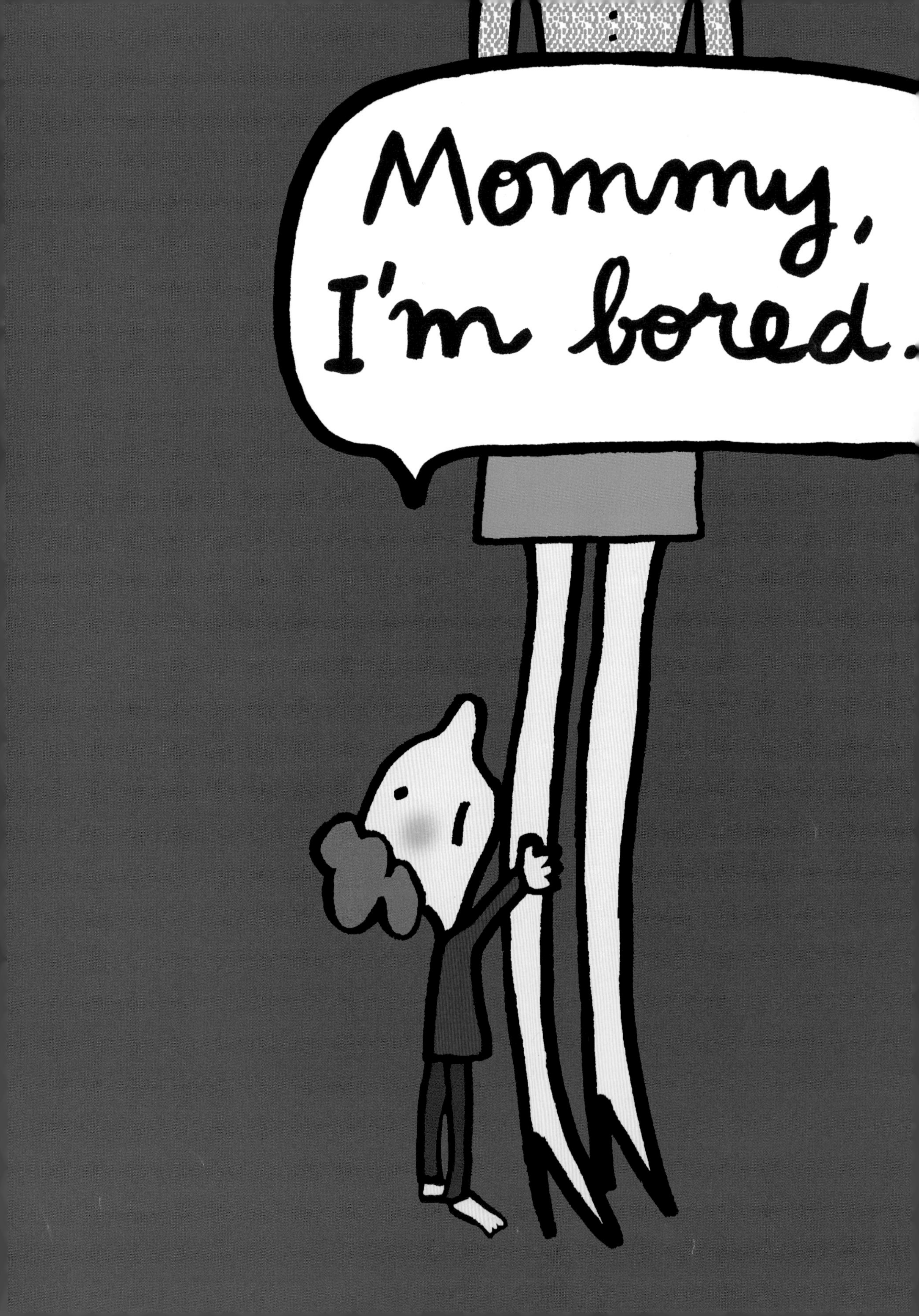
Mommy, I'm bored...

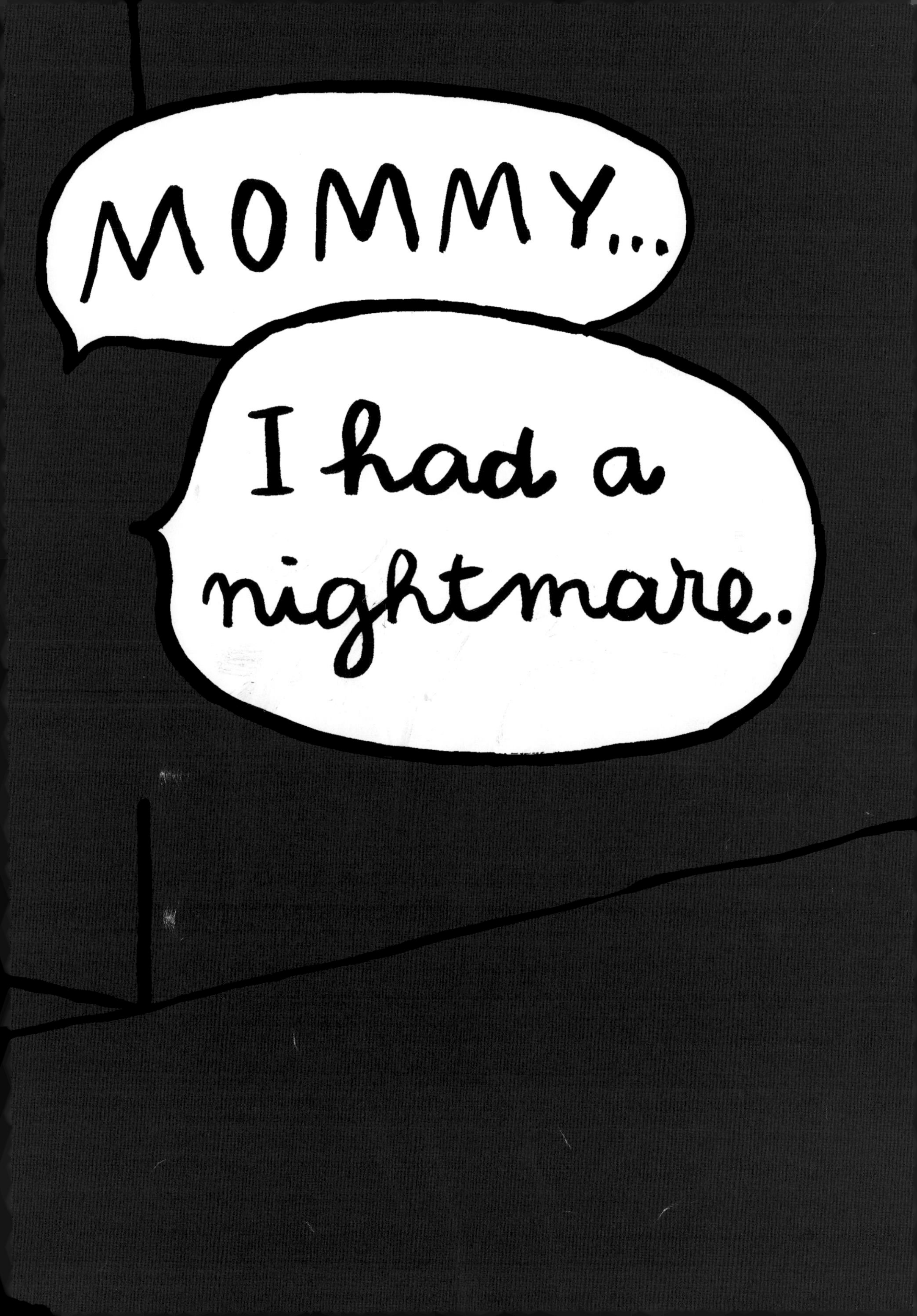
MOMMY...
I had a nightmare.

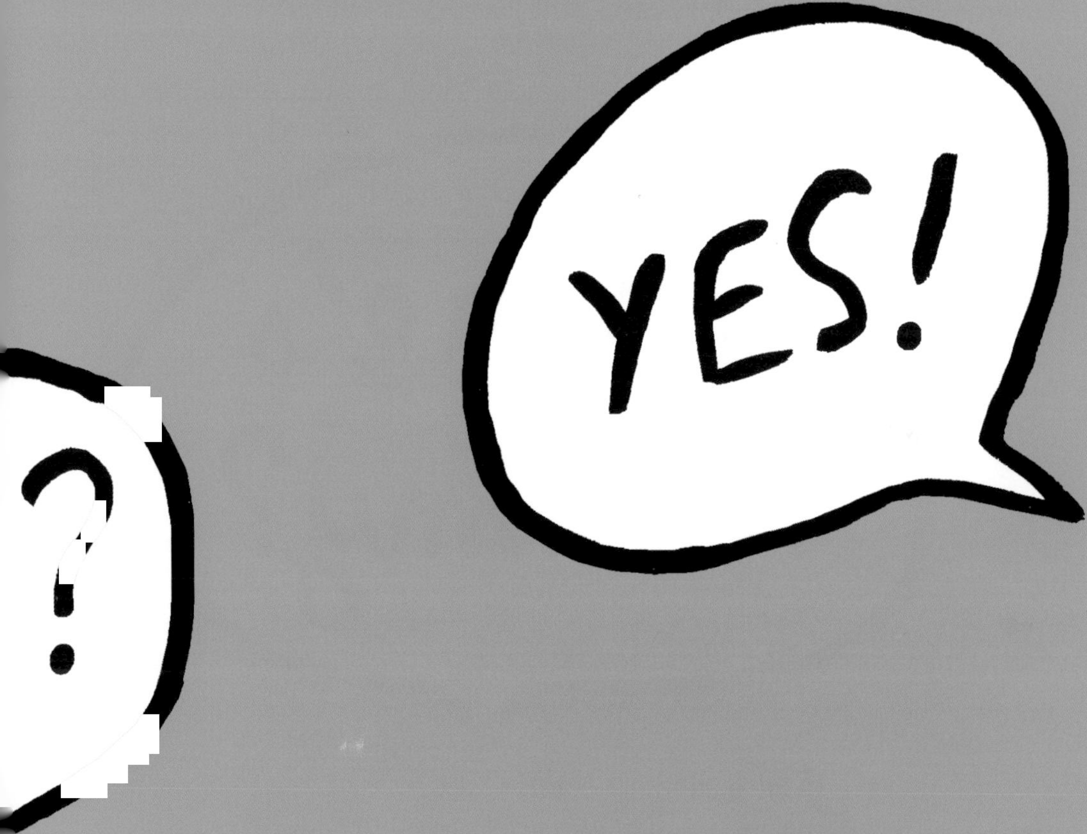
?
YES!

Farrar Straus Giroux Books for Young Readers
175 Fifth Avenue, New York 10010

Originally published in French by l'école des loisirs as *Maman dans tes bras*
Text and illustrations by Soledad Bravi
© 2014, l'école des loisirs, Paris
Translation copyright © 2016 by Franck Goldberg
All rights reserved
Printed in China by Macmillan Production (Asia) Ltd.,
Kowloon Bay, Hong Kong (vendor code: 10)
First American edition, 2016
1 3 5 7 9 10 8 6 4 2

mackids.com

Library of Congress Cataloging-in-Publication Data
Bravi, Soledad, author, illustrator
    [Maman dans tes bras. English]
    Mommy, pick me up / Soledad Bravi. — First edition.
        pages cm
    Originally published in French by l'école des loisirs in 2014 under title: Maman dans tes bras.
    Summary: "A humorous story about a little boy and all the things he wants his mommy to
help him with"— Provided by publisher.
    ISBN 978-0-374-30268-9 (hardback)
    [1. Mother and child—Fiction.   2. Humorous stories.]   I. Title.

PZ7.1.S667Mo 2016
[E]—dc23
                                                                    2015013302

Our books may be purchased in bulk for promotional, educational, or business use. Please
contact your local bookseller or the Macmillan Corporate and Premium Sales Department at
(800) 221-7945 ext. 5442 or by e-mail at MacmillanSpecialMarkets@macmillan.com.

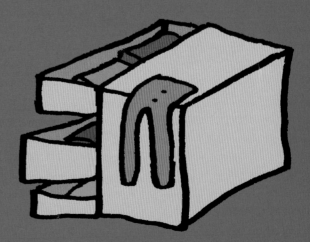